INTRODUCTION

Long ago, the historic county of Medland was made up of four separate regions. These divisions can now only be found on ancient maps, but people living in the old North, South, East and West Quarters remain loyal to their own area.

One example of how the traditional keen rivalry still survives is the County Cup, a season-long soccer tournament for schools. Group games have already been played, and the new Quarter Champions are about to clash in the two-legged, semi-final stage of the competition.

The eventual Cup Winners will receive the much-prized silver trophy and earn the right to call themselves the County Champions – the top team in Medland.

THE COUNTY OF MEDLAND

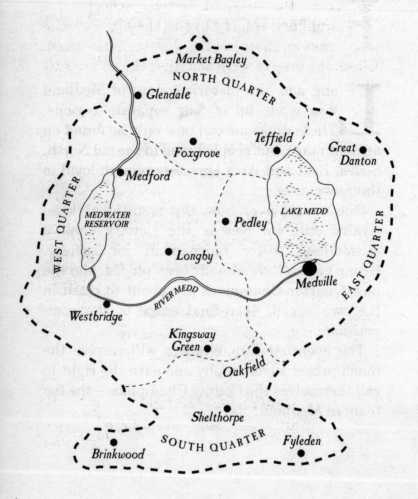

Market Bagley

NORTH QUARTER

Glendale

Teffield

Great
Danton

Foxgrove

WEST QUARTER

Medford

MEDWATER
RESERVOIR

LAKE MEDD

Pedley

Longby

RIVER MEDD

Medville

EAST QUARTER

Westbridge

Kingsway
Green

Oakfield

Shelthorpe

Fyleden

SOUTH QUARTER

Brinkwood

QUARTER CHAMPIONS

From the original sixteen schools that qualified to play in the County Cup this season, these are the Quarter Champions. Check the map to see where the schools are situated.

NORTH QUARTER

Glendale Community School

EAST QUARTER (Joint)

Lakeview High School, Medville

Medville Comprehensive School

SOUTH QUARTER

St Wystan's Comprehensive
School, Brinkwood

WEST QUARTER

Westbridge Community College

MEET THE TEAMS

The semi-final knockout stage of the County Cup involves some of the best young footballers in Medland. The players have been eagerly looking forward to the matches ever since the draw was made before the Christmas holidays.

SEMI-FINAL DRAW		
SOUTH QUARTER	V	EAST QUARTER
WEST QUARTER	V	NORTH QUARTER

Ties to be played over two legs on 31 January and 28 February

Winners decided on aggregate scores. If goals are level, the tie goes to a play-off, plus extra time and penalties if necessary.

Let's concentrate here on the **West v North semi-final.** Meet the teams on the next few pages, replay the highlights of their group action and then enjoy all the excitement of the County Cup.

WESTBRIDGE COMMUNITY COLLEGE

Large comprehensive school in the town of Westbridge on the River Medd in the West Quarter.

Headteacher: *Mr Walter Hooper*
P.E. teacher: *Mr Doug Griffiths*
School colours: *white shirts, black shorts and socks*
Year 7 soccer captain: *Emerson Marshall*
Usual team formation: *4–1–3–2 (attacking sweeper system)*

Year 7 soccer squad:

Adam Trent

Dan Cross   Emerson Marshall   Brad Gibson   Craig Dalton

(Kenny)
William Kennedy

(King Kong)
Eddie Atkins   Richard Congdon   Sam Lucas

(Bax)
Iain Baxter   Oliver Yates

plus: Mark Palmer, Ajay Jethwa, Jacob Roberts, (Bob) Dylan Small, Jim Chalmers, Dean Matthews, Andy Thornton, Yagnesh Sharma (absent)

I reckon we've done pretty well to reach this stage of the County Cup. We had to play every group game away from home because the soccer pitches were wrecked by all the building work on a big sports hall. We're thinking of calling ourselves the Westbridge Wanderers!

No idea yet what's going to happen about the semifinal. It won't be fair if we've got to play both legs up at Glendale. The pitches are gradually recovering, but the flooding last term didn't exactly help.

Player—wise, the news is also mixed. The loss of Yagnesh, who's away in India for the first leg, is made up for by the timely arrival of Big Ollie. We're expecting tons of goals from him, so watch out Glendale! (Extra warning for our Cup opponents: tangling with defender Dan Cross can seriously damage your health!)

We may have our problems, but one thing's for sure. Life's never dull if you ride the College convoy. So get out your maps and wander with us on our travels. The roads will lead all the way to the Cup Final!

GLENDALE COMMUNITY SCHOOL

L arge comprehensive school in market town of Glendale in the North Quarter.

Headteacher: *Mrs Margaret Burrows*
Head of P.E. Dept: *Mr Brian Fisher*
School colours: *royal blue shirts, shorts and socks*
Year 7 soccer captain: *Paul Stevens*
Usual team formation: *4–2–4*

Year 7 soccer squad

Ian Jacobs (Crackers)

(Batty)   (Dips)
Richard Curtis Paul Stevens Tom Bateman Dipesh Patel

(Wainy)
Hanif Khan Alex Wainwright

(Giant)   (Leggy)
Nick Green   Harry Taylor Chris Kemp Tim Lamb

plus: Scott Harris, Carl Simpson, Jeff Smith, David Nash, Robbie Jones, Gary Thomas

CAPTAIN'S
Notes...

Having to write more of these notes is one job I'm very happy to do again — it means we're still in the Cup! We sure cut it fine. Our last crucial group game against the Foxes could easily have gone either way, but we're through and that's the main thing. We can't wait now to get to grips with Westbridge College in the semis.

I gather they've got pitch problems, which should work to our advantage, especially if both legs have to be played here at Glendale. We're still unbeaten at home this season.

New Year's Resolution for the team — stop giving away soft goals! We have no trouble scoring goals — our main strike force, Giant and Kempy, got nearly thirty between them by Christmas — but we're sometimes a bit too reckless going forward and can get caught on the break. At least our first-choice keeper, Crackers, is fit again after damaging his ankle last term.

Hope you'll come along and support us and help us reach the Final. This is where all the action is!

13

CUP TRAIL

West Quarter

FINAL GROUP TABLE

	P	W	D	L	Goals F	A	(GD)	Pts
Westbridge	3	2	1	0	7	4	(+3)	7
Riverside	3	1	2	0	8	7	(+1)	5
Hillcrest	3	0	2	1	5	7	(−2)	2
Kingsway Green	3	0	1	2	4	6	(−2)	1

Group Highlights

. . . 'Griff wouldn't dare send me off,' Dan Cross sneered. 'I reckon we'll be able to get away with murder this season.'

***

. . . *The boy's well named,' frowned Mr Griffiths, the College teacher. 'Cross by name, cross by nature.'*

***

. . . Dan's short, fast-burning fuse ignited and College's first Cup match suddenly exploded into life. Penalty!

***

. . . *'Don't you think you're in enough trouble already, Dan, without playing truant as well?' said Mr Griffiths. 'You've been banned from the Cup!'*

***

. . . 'All our pitches are flooded,' said Emerson, the College captain. 'The only game we could have played at Westbridge is water polo!'

***

. . . *The College goal was a fluke. Sam sliced his shot but saw it take a deflection off a defender's shoulder, flip up against the bar then ricochet down and hit the Hillcrest goalie on the head before rolling into the net.*

***

. . . 'I'm afraid there's a fixture clash,' said the head of the College's P.E. department. 'I want three of the footballers to run in the cross-country races instead of playing in the Cup.'

***

. . . *'I gather things are so bad at Westbridge, you've had to go into the transfer market and sign up a new star player,' joked the Riverside teacher.*

***

. . . Newcomer Oliver Yates outjumped the tall centre-back for a cross and headed the ball down to Yagnesh who struck it first time past the gawping goalkeeper.

***

. . . *'Might just play for my Sunday team after Christmas,' Dan muttered. 'I've had a right bellyful of old Griff subbing me.'*

***

. . . 'Er, I'm not sure I'll be here to play in the first leg of the Semis,' admitted Yagnesh sheepishly. 'My parents are taking me on a trip to India!'

CUP TRAIL

North Quarter

FINAL GROUP TABLE

	P	W	D	L	Goals F	A	(GD)	Pts
Glendale	3	2	1	0	9	5	(+4)	7
Foxgrove	3	2	0	1	8	3	(+5)	6
Mkt Bagley	3	0	2	1	3	6	(−3)	2
Teffield	3	0	1	2	4	10	(−6)	1

Group Highlights

. . . 'We beat Glendale 4–2 last month, so they're sure to be out for revenge when we meet them later in the Cup,' said the Foxes captain.

***

. . . *Glendale's substitute swaggered onto the pitch, sleeves rolled up to show everyone he meant business. 'Right, let's sort this lot out now I'm on,' Carl demanded.*

***

. . . 'Think I've just been hit by a jumbo jet,' mumbled the Baggies captain groggily after his mid-air collision with Carl.

***

. . . *'You're rubbish, Crackers!' Carl sneered. 'My granny could've saved them two goals you let in.'*

***

. . . 'I'd rather we lost trying to play good football than kicked our way through the County Cup,' sighed Paul, Glendale's captain.

***

. . . *'I bet that moron will get a double suspension now,' chuckled one of the subs after Carl was sent off. 'Banned from football and from school!'*

***

. . . 'They're all against me,' Carl fumed, throwing his muddy boots against the cloak-room wall. Then he went round all the coats, dipping his hands into the pockets to see what he could find.

***

. . . *We only need a draw against Glendale today to be Quarter Champions,' said Lynx, the Foxes skilful midfielder. 'That's what makes us favourites.'*

***

. . . Just before half-time, Crackers' injured ankle gave way and he crumpled to the ground, helpless, as the ball was scooped over the crossbar.

***

. . . *In the final minute of the game, the ball fell at the feet of the Foxes captain and he hammered it through the forest of bodies. Nashy, Glendale's sub goalie, never even saw it coming until the last split second.*

***

. . . 'Knowing Carl, he might even try and make us lose the semi-final just to get his own back,' said Nashy gloomily.

FORM GUIDE

Glendale

In second place behind Foxgrove in ten-school North Quarter league. Scoring plenty of goals, but attacking policy has also cost them a few league points due to lack of cover in defence. Still on course for a cup double, reaching the semi-final of the local cup too.

Leading goalscorers: Taylor – 16, Kemp – 11, Green – 8

County Cup goalscorers: Kemp – 3, Taylor – 2, Green – 1, Khan – 1, Patel – 1, Simpson – 1

Westbridge

Joint top of nine-school West Quarter league table with Riverside. Good defensive record with effective sweeper system, despite having to play away from home all the time because of poor state of the College pitches. Surprise defeat in quarter-final of the local cup.

Leading goalscorers: Baxter – 8, Lucas – 7, Sharma – 6

County Cup goalscorers: Sharma – 2, Baxter – 1, Lucas – 1, Congdon – 1, Small – 1, Yates – 1

. . . Right, you now have all the information you need to make a choice. Which school do you think will reach the County Cup Final? Or perhaps, who do you most want to get through? Read on and find out what happens . . .

WEST v NORTH

Saturday 17 January
k.o. 10.30 a.m.
Referee: Mr D. Griffiths

. . . scene: Riverside School, Medford – where some of the Cup semi-finalists meet up with one another as they represent their respective Quarters in the first area match of the new term . . .

Five minutes into the game a left-wing cross curled high into the goalmouth and North's beanpole striker outjumped everyone to head the ball into the net.

West keeper Adam Trent was not best pleased.

So how are we going to stop him doing that again?

It's too late by the time the ball comes over. We'll just have to try and cut out the service from the wings

That was easier said than done. Emerson didn't know that both the North wingers were also teammates of the goalscorer at school. Nor was the captain of Westbridge College aware at the time that they all played for Glendale, College's opponents in the semi-final of the County Cup.

The Glendale trio were busy celebrating.

Great goal, Giant

Couldn't miss when Leggy drops the ball right on my head.

So why don't you score every time Nickandme do that? You'd notch up about ten goals a game!

Goals in football, however, don't come as freely as they do in basketball. Try as they might, the North attackers could not repeat the magic formula for creating goals, thanks mainly to good solid defending by the home team and also to two excellent saves by Adam.

HALF-TIME

You're making it look as if they're top of the quarter league, not us. Our attack's hardly seen the ball yet. So go out there this half and show them how you can play.

The manager's criticism stung the boys' pride and the second half told a different story. West turned a 0–1 deficit into a 3–1 victory with three stunning goals.

West captain Robbo dribbled through to equalize...

1.

College's new striker, Oliver Yates, making his debut for the West Quarter, shot them in front...

2.

...and finally, Big Norm got sweet revenge over Giant by timing his run better to meet a corner and head home for the third.

3.

Full-time—and someone makes a point of shaking hands with Emerson after the match.

Well played, you deserved to win today in the end. I gather you're Emerson.

You gather right—who are you?

Paul Stevens—captain of Glendale. Just wanted to find out where we'll be playing the first leg.

Still a secret. We're wanting to keep everybody guessing a bit longer.

The truth was that Emerson himself didn't know either. His P.E. teacher, Mr Griffiths, had not yet made the final decision about whether the College soccer pitches were safe enough to use after the damage caused by building work and flooding.

Well, see you in a fortnight—somewhere.

Yeah, we'll be there—anywhere.

... let's now take a look behind the scenes at both schools as they prepare for their Cup semi-final — wherever the first leg might be played ...

BANNED

. . . Carl Simpson is changing with Glendale's Year 7 soccer squad for the first time since his sending off in a Cup group game back in November . . .

'How did you get those marks on your back?' asked Mr Fisher.

Carl quickly pulled the soccer shirt over his head and turned round to face the sports teacher. 'What marks?' he mumbled.

'Looked like long scratches.'

'Oh, them,' Carl said with a shrug. 'Must've been when I fell off my bike in the holidays. Had a new bike for Christmas, see, and I wasn't used to it.'

Mr Fisher was Carl's form tutor as well. Although Carl had been involved in all sorts of trouble in his first term at Glendale, on and off the pitch, the teacher was willing to give him the opportunity of making a fresh start. He also wanted to show the boy that he was concerned about his welfare.

'They still seem rather red to me. Can I have another look at them?'

Carl pulled a face and shifted uneasily from one bare foot to another. 'It's OK, Mr Fisher, honest. They don't hurt or nothing, really. Almost forgot about them, like.'

The teacher sighed. 'All right, Carl, if you say so. Finish getting changed now. I want you out on the pitch in five minutes.'

'Um . . . I *will* be getting a game on Saturday, won't I?'

'You'll be in the squad, yes, I told you so. And I'll try and put you on at some point, but I can't promise.'

'What about the Cup match next week?'

The teacher stared at him. 'That's different, as you know. You have to serve a two-match ban in the competition and you've only missed one.'

The boy flushed, glancing round as he sensed that others were listening. 'But you said I could start playing again this term,' he persisted.

Mr Fisher, too, realized they had an audience. The changing room had become very quiet, with every ear cocked in their direction. 'Look, Carl, I'm sorry, but the County Cup is a separate issue altogether. I'm afraid I can't pick you for the first leg and that's all there is to it.'

Carl slumped down onto the bench, head down, and angrily tugged on his socks. When he thought that nobody was looking, he wiped his sleeve across his eyes. 'Not fair,' he muttered to himself. 'They've all got it in for me. Well, I'll show 'em soon. Just wait . . .'

Carl was very subdued during the short lunchtime practice session, not even raising the effort to abuse anyone who complained about a misplaced pass or his failure to chase after the ball to stop it going out of play.

'Never seen him so quiet,' said Leggy.

'I prefer him like this,' smirked Wainy, who'd been more pleased than most when Carl was suspended last term. Alex Wainwright had been one of the victims of Carl's bullying behaviour right through their primary school days.

'Do you reckon he's ill or something?'

Wainy shook his head. 'He's just sulking 'cos he can't play in the Cup. Serves him right.'

'Give him a chance.'

'Why should I? He never gave me one.'

'But he can play OK when he really tries,' Leggy argued. 'I mean, he's got a good strong left foot.'

'Yeah, I know,' Wainy said with feeling. 'He's kicked me with it often enough in the past.'

Carl demonstrated its power just a minute later, the one decent touch he had of the ball

during the whole session. It rolled loose his way
as he stood, seemingly uninterested, on the edge
of the penalty area and he suddenly swung his
left boot. Goalkeeper Ian Jacobs was rooted
helplessly to the spot as the ball sped past him.

'On yer bike, Crackers!' laughed Paul Stevens,
the captain. 'Go and fetch it.'

The goalie didn't bother. He simply picked up
the nearest ball from behind the posts instead.
'He belted it – he can fetch it,' Crackers
grunted. 'I'm not doing the legwork for that
nutter.'

'You're not his greatest fan, are you?' Paul
chuckled.

'The feeling's mutual. C'mon, you don't want
him in the side either, admit it.'

'I do if he scores goals like that one.'

'What, at the expense of team spirit?' Crackers retorted. 'If Fisher picks him again, I reckon he wants his head examining.'

Without apparently feeling the need to seek an urgent appointment with his doctor, however, the teacher named Carl among the substitutes for Glendale's first league game of the new term. They were at home to Market Bagley, a team that had already held them to a draw in the Cup. A few of the Baggies had good reason to remember Carl's brief appearance on that occasion. They still had the scars as souvenirs.

HOME OR AWAY?

. . . Westbridge have a problem player of their own, Dan Cross, besides still being homeless . . .

'I'm fed up of travelling to every game,' grumbled Kenny, the College sweeper, or *libero* as Mr Griffiths liked to call him. The soccer coach was a big fan of Italian football.

'Yeah, this'll be the third time we've had to trek across to Kingsway Green this season,' said Adam, the team's goalkeeper. 'No wonder people are nicknaming us the Westbridge Wanderers.'

'So long as they don't confuse us with Dan's Sunday side,' said Emerson, pulling a face. 'I don't want us getting mixed up with that rabble.'

'Watch it, captain!' retorted Sam Lucas. 'I play for Wanderers as well, remember.'

Emerson's frown turned into a broad grin. 'I know, Sam, I was just joking. Has Dan been sent off again lately?'

The striker ignored this taunt and scuffed at a clump of mud in the penalty area. The footballers were inspecting one of the College pitches before their training session in the new sports hall. 'It's not *too* bad this end,' he said. 'Reckon it's just about OK to use now, don't you?'

Emerson nodded. 'What do you think, Adam? You're the one who'd have to go diving about on all the ruts.'

'Not if you defenders did your job properly, I wouldn't,' he smirked before addressing the question more seriously. 'Well, it's loads better than before Christmas, that's for sure, but . . .'

'Watch out – here comes Griff,' Kenny interrupted him.

'C'mon, you lot,' called the teacher. 'I thought you'd all be changed by now.'

'Just checking the pitch, Mr Griffiths,' replied Emerson. 'We're hoping it might be fit for the Cup.'

'So am I,' he said, coming up to join them. 'I'm going to make a final decision early next week about the semi-final. I'd love us to be at home, but it's only fair to give Glendale time to alter their travel plans.'

'You mean, we might not have to play both legs at their place?'

'That's right. I sorted things out with their teacher at the area game. They've agreed to let the first leg be at Riverside instead, if necessary. It isn't so far for Glendale to travel, so they're quite happy.'

The footballers raced inside to tell their teammates the good news, while Mr Griffiths had another look at the pitch himself. 'Might all depend on the weather,' he sighed, peering suspiciously up at the sky.

Five minutes later, as his squad went through a series of stretching exercises during the warm-up session, the teacher counted only fifteen bodies. The four absentees included Yagnesh Sharma, who was away in India, but Mr Griffiths wasn't at all surprised to find that Dan Cross was missing too.

'So what's up with Dan, does anybody know?' he said during a short break. 'I've scarcely seen him this term.'

Scarce was probably the right word for it. Dan was very good at making himself scarce – a past master at playing truant. The teacher knew it was a silly question as soon as he asked it. No-one was going to split on Dan, whatever they thought about his actions. They didn't dare.

'Well, if any of you *do* see him around,' he continued to break the lengthening silence, 'tell him from me that I can't very well pick him for the Cup next week if he doesn't show his face at school – and more importantly, keep it here all day, every day.'

Mr Griffiths was pleased with the commitment shown by the players who *were* present. They were keen to be chosen for Saturday's league match in the hope that a good performance would help them to keep their place in the starting eleven for the Cup.

Oliver Yates' team won the little five-a-side tournament that followed various ball-skills practices. They traded goals at either end but always managed to score more than they conceded.

'Great goal, Big Ollie,' grinned Emerson after the powerful striker smashed the winner past Adam in the deciding game. 'Hope you've saved some goals for Saturday. We need the three points to keep pace with Riverside at the top of the league.'

'Sure,' chuckled Oliver, slapping Emerson's raised hand in salute. 'Plenty more where that came from, no sweat.'

TAKE ONE GAME AT A TIME

. . . Saturday 24 January: important league points are at stake for both schools before they hit the Cup trail again – here's a summary of all the goals in the North . . .

Glendale v Market Bagley

★ *Scoreflash: Glendale 0 – 1 Market Bagley*
The Baggies shock the home side with a goal in the third minute. Twin strikers Luke Wilde and Daniel West play a one-two inside the penalty area and West slides the ball wide of Ian Jacobs' dive into the net . . .

★ *Scoreflash: Glendale 1 – 1 Market Bagley*
Glendale equalize midway through the first half when left-winger Tim Lamb centres for giant striker Harry Taylor to nod home from close-range . . .

★ *Scoreflash: Glendale 2 – 1 Market Bagley*
The visitors' defenders are still blaming one another for the poor marking that allowed the equalizer when the Blues score again. Right-winger Nick Green this time provides the cross for Taylor's head . . .

**Half-time:
Glendale 2 – 1 Market Bagley**

★ *Scoreflash: Glendale 2 – 2 Market Bagley*
Straight after the interval, Wilde is given the freedom of the park to run through the middle of the defence and fire the ball past Jacobs . . .

★ *Scoreflash: Glendale 3 – 2 Market Bagley*
Substitute Carl Simpson forces a good save out of the Baggies keeper to win a corner, the first of four in a row. This spell of heavy pressure brings its due reward when centre-back Paul Stevens finds the net from the edge of the area. A rare goal indeed for the Glendale captain . . .

★ *Scoreflash: Glendale 4 – 2 Market Bagley*
The home victory is assured five minutes from
time after the Baggies captain, Duncan 'Ding-
Dong' Bell, trips Simpson just inside the area.
A flash of temper from Simpson earns him a
lecture from referee, Mr Fisher. Taylor is given
the honour of taking the penalty kick and sends
the keeper the wrong way to complete his hat-
trick.

Final score: Glendale 4 – 2 Market Bagley

. . . followed by edited highlights of College's game in the West Quarter . . .

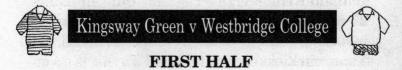

Kingsway Green v Westbridge College

FIRST HALF

4 mins: first shot of the match is saved by College keeper Adam Trent, holding on to a low drive from home team captain Kyle Richards

7 mins: only a last-ditch intervention by his opposing captain, centre-back Emerson Marshall, thwarts Richards again with Trent out of position

10 mins: Kingsway Green keeper Gary Rees at last has a touch of the ball, but only to fish it out of his net. He failed to get near the fierce volley from College number nine Oliver Yates

★*Scorecheck: Kingsway Green 0 – 1 Westbridge*

13 mins: Rees more successful this time, saving well from Iain Baxter, College's top goalscorer
18 mins: College caught stretched at the back by a breakaway raid. Trent and full-back Craig Dalton scramble the ball away between them
22 mins: Marshall kicks a shot off the goal-line

23 mins: goalmouth scramble following a corner is finally cleared by College libero William Kennedy

 27 mins: slick move up the left by the visitors involving Dalton, Kennedy and Sam Lucas, but Yates miskicks in front of goal

30 mins: Kingsway Green's number ten is equally guilty of a bad miss, scooping hurried shot over bar

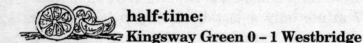 **half-time:**
Kingsway Green 0 – 1 Westbridge

SECOND HALF

2 mins: College's keeper straight into the thick of the action, pulling off dramatic double save.

 8 mins: Kingsway Green now dominating game but are missing the cool finishing of leading scorer, Didier Pires, who has returned home to France. Midfielder Callum Briggs slices shot wide from five metres out

 11 mins: Marshall makes crucial block to prevent almost certain equalizer

15 mins: College's first dangerous attack of the second half ends with Lucas lobbing Rees, only to see ball land on top of netting

19 mins: Briggs injured in tackle by Richard Congdon and limps off

 21 mins: substitute Ben Lynton almost makes Congdon regret his foul, slipping ball through midfielder's legs but then striking shot off target

 24 mins: home team find the net at last but at the wrong end – Lynton unluckily deflects a shot from Lucas past his own keeper

★ *Scorecheck: Kingsway Green 0 – 2 Westbridge*

 28 mins: save of the match by Trent, performing a spectacular leap to turn header over crossbar

30 mins: Richards strikes College post in injury time and Trent recovers to block rebound effort and keep another clean sheet

Full-time: Kingsway Green 0 – 2 Wesbridge

. . . let's get to know the two Cup captains a little better . . .

FLOODLIGHT FOCUS

... on **Paul Stevens**

school	Glendale
other teams	Dale Dynamos (Sunday League) North Quarter
position	centre-back (midfield on Sundays)
best foot forward	right-footed
age	12 years 4 months
build	taller than average
nickname	Stevo
ambition	to be a professional footballer
pets	none
family	one sister
superstitions	wear lucky underpants in matches!
hobbies	football, computers, teasing kid sister
so embarrassing!	not wearing pants once when shorts got ripped!

favourites

school subject	P.E.
football team	Glasgow Rangers (Dad's Scottish)
book	any Terry Pratchett books – they're all brilliant
TV programme	*Only Fools and Horses*
music	any pop music
food	crisps
drink	milk – don't like any hot drinks
word/saying	brilliant

FLOODLIGHT FOCUS

... on **Emerson Marshall**

school	Westbridge College
other teams	River Boys Under-12s (Sunday League)
	West Quarter Area side
position	centre defence and captain
best foot forward	right
age	11 years 11 months
build	big for my age
nickname	The Lawman
ambition	want to be a fast bowler for West Indies
pets	we've only got boring tropical fish
family	brother and sister
superstitions	always call 'Heads' at the toss
hobbies	football and cricket
so embarrassing!	being hit for six by my younger brother

favourites

school subject	games and maths
football team	Jamaica
book	Roald Dahl books still make me laugh
TV programme	Test Match cricket highlights

music	Reggae
food	chicken and chips
drink	Coke
word/saying	total respect

CAPTAINCY

It is a great honour to be chosen as captain, but the job is about far more than just tossing a coin at the start of a match.

Want to know what it takes to be a good captain? Take a few tips from me.

✓ The captain doesn't have to be the best player – he needs other skills too

✓ He needs to be a strong character and have the respect of his teammates

✓ He should try and lead by example, both on and off the pitch

✓ Communicate – talk to teammates during game, inspire, praise, encourage, instruct and criticize if necessary

✓ Part of the captain's duties is to be the link between the coach and players

✓ He may help to decide tactics - or even team selection - and see they are carried out in the game

✓ Be ready to make decisions and even change tactics during match

✓ And last but not least, the toss! Have a clear idea what to do if it's won

HEADS!

ON OR OFF?

... the Westbridge P.E. teacher, Mr Griffiths, has a tricky decision to make – whether or not to try and play the first leg of the Cup semi-final at home ...

'On me head, man!' cried Oliver.

Richard Congdon steadied himself before crossing the ball, but the centre was too high even for Oliver to get his head to it. Fortunately, Sam was steaming in behind him and met the dropping ball smack on his forehead. He sent it back across the face of the goal into the top corner of the net.

'Wicked ball, King Kong!' Sam shouted in delight.

'Yeah, apart from the fact it was meant for Big Ollie,' he confessed.

'Doesn't matter who gets on the end of it,' laughed Bax. 'It's great having Big Ollie here now as the main target man. While defences are panicking, trying to mark him, me and Sam can sneak in unnoticed.'

'It'll be even better when Yagnesh gets back from India,' said Sam. 'He can put over some wicked crosses with that left foot of his. Team's a bit unbalanced without him on the left.'

'Well, we'll still have to manage without him for the first leg,' sighed Bax. 'He's not due back till early Feb.'

The Year 7 squad, still minus Dan, was practising on the biggest of the College's soccer pitches, the only one that had been undamaged by the building work. It was too large for their age-group to play a proper match on, but they were hopeful that the others might be fit for use by the weekend. Mr Griffiths was inspecting them again now.

'Fingers crossed,' said Kenny as the teacher wandered thoughtfully back towards them.

'OK, lads, gather round,' Mr Griffiths called out. 'I've decided we'll risk it!'

A loud cheer erupted from the players. 'Yeeesss!' cried Emerson. 'Magic! We're unbeaten at home this season.'

'That's only 'cos we haven't played at home yet,' laughed Bax.

'Yes, we have. We tried out that new little pitch once. It was all boggy, remember?'

'I do,' put in Kenny. 'I scored with a shot from our own half.'

'Well, this one won't be boggy, I can assure you of that,' the teacher said. 'I think the weather might be turning colder, but unless it freezes hard, we should be all right.'

Sadly, it proved to be the wrong decision. The temperatures dropped lower than expected and there was even a light sprinkling of snow on the Friday evening. As soon as Mr Griffiths looked out of his bedroom window on the Saturday morning, his heart sank. The front lawn was white-over. And when he arrived at Westbridge College, he saw straight away that the match could not go ahead. The ruts had frozen into hard, dangerous ridges, making the risk of injury too great.

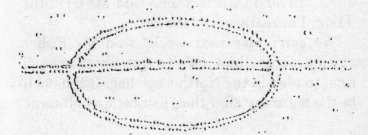

Mr Griffiths stood by the school gate to give people the bad news as they arrived. He was still speaking to Mr Riley, the referee and West Quarter manager, when the Glendale convoy turned up. Only their teacher, Mr Fisher, bothered to get out of his car.

'Sorry, Brian, I'm afraid you've had a wasted journey,' Mr Riley began.

'No need to tell me, I'd already guessed,' he replied, not even greeting Mr Griffiths. Brian Fisher was clearly annoyed and didn't mind who knew it. 'What are *your* pitches like at Riverside this morning, Jeff?'

Jeff Riley was in an awkward position. 'Well, I haven't actually had a chance to check,' he said, 'but I guess they might have been playable.'

'Right, well I don't want any repeat of this nonsense,' said Mr Fisher. 'I insist we play the game either at Glendale or Riverside. Which is it to be?'

The West Quarter teachers glanced at each other. 'Riverside, it is, then,' said Mr Griffiths. 'Look, I'm really sorry about . . .'

'We can't play next week,' said Mr Fisher, cutting across him. 'We've got another semi-final to play in the North Cup then. It'll have to be the Saturday after that, just before half-term.'

Several of the College players were standing nearby, listening, and Bax was the first to see the silver lining in the postponement. 'You know what this means, don't you?' he said, breaking into a wide grin.

'Yeah, we've all got out of bed early for nothing,' grunted Sam.

'Not that – it means we'll be at full strength for the first leg now.'

'Doubt it. Dan says he's not gonna play for the school again.'

'I'm not talking about Dan. Yaggy should be back with us by then.'

Emerson suddenly realized something else about the new date. 'Hey! The game will be on my birthday now, the fourteenth of February. We'll have to win – don't want my party spoiled by losing.'

'Watch out, Glendale, you could be in for it that day,' laughed Kenny. 'If we hit form, it could be the Saint Valentine's Day Massacre!'

. . . Doesn't sound like the two teachers will be sending each other Valentine cards, though, does it? There'll be no love lost between them now . . .

SEMI-FINAL: FIRST LEG

WESTBRIDGE v GLENDALE

(at Riverside Comprehensive, Medford)

Saturday 14 February
k.o. 10.30 a.m.
Referee: Mr J. Riley

. . . St Valentine's Day dawns bright and clear, and both teams are at full strength – apart from lacking the services of the two hard men, Dan (absent) and Carl (suspended) . . .

As soon as the teachers left the changing room, the College players began singing a silly verse that Kenny had made up in the car as they drove past Medwater Reservoir:

Roses are red, violets are blue.
We've got a message, specially for you.
The water's deep, the water's wet.
Listen, Glendale, to what you'll get!

At this point, Kenny stood on one of the benches to lead the chanting.

'Give us an M . . .' he demanded loudly.

'M,' they chorused.

'Give us an A . . .'

'A.'

'Give us an S . . .'

'S.'

And so it went on as the Glendale players were forced to listen to their fate being spelt out as they changed. Kenny forgot to double the middle 'S' in the word, but the final message came across loud and clear.

'And what are Glendale gonna get?' he shouted at the top of his voice.

'MASSACRED!' his teammates screamed back at him.

Jeers and taunts were hurled back at them from the other side of the changing room, but Glendale had nothing ready prepared to mount an appropriate counter attack.

'Reckon that's one-nil to us already,' grinned Emerson.

When the real score became 1–0 shortly after the kick-off, the Glendale players might have been excused if fears of a possible massacre did fleetingly cross their minds. As a Blues' attack broke down outside the Westbridge penalty area, the ball was pumped over the halfway line, catching both full-backs out of position too far forward. Paul and Batty, the captain's partner in central defence, found themselves exposed, outnumbered four against two by the lightning raid.

Sam switched the ball out to Bax on the right and his low cross was aimed at Oliver in the middle. Batty was fooled completely when the number nine cleverly stepped over the ball at the last moment, leaving it to run on to a team-mate in space behind him. Yagnesh Sharma was unmarked and unhurried – and his shot was unstoppable. All the goalkeeper had to do was disentangle the ball from the netting.

'Welcome back, Yaggy!' cried Sam, jumping onto the scorer's back and toppling them both to the ground.

'That's an extra birthday present for the captain,' Yagnesh giggled, scrambling to his feet before Big Ollie could land on him too. 'All the way from India!'

To their credit, Glendale didn't let the early setback affect them too much. They were confident in their own ability to score goals and had won several games this season after falling behind. For a while, it looked as if they were playing at home, mounting a number of attacks up both wings and pressing College back on to the defensive.

Emerson made sure that Oliver came back into his own penalty box to counter Giant's height at set-pieces, and keeper Adam Trent wasn't afraid to leave his line to catch high  crosses or punch the ball clear. Adam was a good shot-stopper, too, as he demonstrated midway through the half when he blocked a well-struck effort from right-winger Nick Green.

Adam's opposite number at the other end of the pitch had a relatively quiet first half after that opening goal. Crackers had a few back-passes to deal with, kicking the ball away cleanly, and a header from Oliver that was straight at him, but little else troubled him apart from a shot by Bax that fizzed just wide of the left-hand post.

By contrast, Adam had to endure several more anxious moments as the Blues strained for an equalizer. Wainy and Leggy linked up to provide striker Chris Kemp with a clear opportunity, which he put over the bar, Giant wasted another chance by misdirecting a header and then Leggy struck a post.

It wasn't until a few minutes before half-time, following more good work from Wainy, that Glendale finally found the net. The small midfielder dribbled past two opponents but as his shot was charged down by a third, the ball ran loose to Nick who steered it past the diving keeper to level the scores.

'Keep it tight at the back second half,' Mr Fisher told his players during the interval, more in hope than expectation. Tight defending was not exactly their strong point. 'If we can hold on to this draw, it'll be a good result to take back to Glendale with us.'

'A win would be even better, Mr Fisher,' Leggy piped up cheekily.

'True,' the teacher agreed, having to smile,

'but I don't think old Crackers here would appreciate you going all out for the winner and then getting caught on the break again.'

The keeper grinned. It was rare for Mr Fisher to use any of their nicknames, a sure sign that he was pleased with their performance so far. 'Sometimes wonder if I've got B.O., the way the rest of you so often leave me on my own,' said Crackers jokingly.

'Nobody dares get close enough to whisper in your ear,' Wainy laughed.

The team talk in the College camp was a rather more serious affair. 'You're letting Glendale come at you too much,' Mr Griffiths said in criticism. 'You've tended to sit back on that early lead and soak up the pressure, but you must try and take the game to them more this half. You'll need another goal or two as a cushion for the second leg.'

'This is supposed to be our home game,' Emerson added as further inspiration to his teammates. 'Let's make it feel like one.'

'I've forgotten what it feels like,' said Kenny sourly. 'Pity away goals don't count double in the County Cup – we're away all the time.'

'Can't be helped, you just have to get on with the job,' replied Mr Griffiths. 'So push forward more now. I want my *libero* to play more of an attacking role, you know that. Play in front of the back four, not behind them as you've been doing most of the first half.'

Kenny took the teacher at his word. There was nothing he enjoyed more than joining the attack. As Quarter cross-country champion, Kenny had the stamina to run up and down the pitch all match if he had to, but he spent much of the second period in Glendale's half. His defensive duties were almost entirely forsaken.

Mr Griffiths shook his head as Kenny pretended not to hear the teacher's repeated calls for him to drop deeper. 'He's gone from one extreme to the other. He's playing as an extra attacker now.'

Kenny's presence up front and his athleticism did cause Glendale a number of problems. Wainy was obliged to play more defensively now to mark Kenny and try to cover his surging runs, but the other College attackers found themselves with a little more space to work than they'd had before. More by accident than design, the balance of the game tilted in favour of Westbridge and Crackers became the busier goalkeeper.

With ten minutes to go, this territorial advantage was reflected in the scoreline. Yagnesh struck again to put his side back in front.

Kenny was involved in the decisive move twice. He started it by winning the ball in midfield then, having laid it off to Sam, kept running to regain possession on the edge of the Glendale penalty area before passing to the scorer. Yagnesh didn't need any further help. He dummied inside the full-back and curled his left-footed shot wide of the advancing Crackers into the far corner of the net.

It proved to be the winning goal. Except for a header from Giant that scraped the bar, Westbridge held on to their lead for the remainder of the game with some degree of comfort.

The two team captains shook hands at the final whistle in mutual respect. 'Well, not quite a massacre, but you probably just about deserved to win overall,' said Paul generously.

Emerson looked a bit sheepish at being reminded of the pre-match taunt. 'Yeah, maybe, but we rode our luck a bit at times too. Bet you lot have scored a few goals this season with an attack like that.'

'Trouble is, we've let a few too many in as well,' Paul grinned. 'I guess we'll just have to make sure we score more than you in the second leg now, that's all.'

Result:	Westbridge 2 v 1 Glendale
	h-t: 1 –1
Scorers:	Sharma (2) Green

Man of the Match: **Yagnesh Sharma**

FLOODLIGHT FOCUS

. . . on **Yagnesh Sharma**

school	*Westbridge College*
other teams	*West Quarter Area side*
position	*left-wing or midfield*
best foot forward	*left-footed*
age	*11 years 8 months*
build	*slim*
nickname	*Yaggy*
ambition	*to become famous!*
pets	*none*
family	*2 brothers, 1 sister – I'm the youngest*
superstitions	*none*
hobbies	*football, tennis, swimming*
so embarrassing!	*to be beaten by my sister once at tennis*

favourites

school subject	*games lessons*
football team	*Leicester City and Aston Villa*
book	*any Goosebumps*
TV programme	*don't know, sorry*
music	*pop*
food	*chicken tikka*
drink	*mineral water*
word/saying	*sorry (I always seem to be apologizing!)*

HALF TERM

. . . get your bike out and let's all go for a ride into the countryside . . .

'Who asked *him* to come with us?'
'I think he invited himself along so he could show off his new bike.'
'Just look at him now. Bet he's trying to impress us.'

Carl Simpson was racing ahead of the other three boys along a narrow country lane south of Glendale. They were making for Three-Quarters-Meet, a well-known beauty spot where three of Medland's four regions came together, overlooking Lake Medd to the East.

'D'yer reckon he'd notice if we suddenly turned off?' grinned Crackers.

'Tempting – but stupid,' said Chris Kemp.

'When he caught up again, he'd probably do the lot of us.'

'Huh! I'd like to see him try,' Crackers grunted, changing into a lower gear as the gradient increased. 'I'm not scared of him.'

'Didn't say I was scared of him. Just a bit wary, that's all.'

'It's OK, Kempy, we know what you mean,' laughed David Nash, the team's utility player, as good in goal as he was in midfield. 'It pays to be a bit wary of old Carl!'

'Only 'cos he's a total nutcase!' added Crackers.

'Well, you should know with a name like yours,' Chris sniggered. 'They say all goalies are crazy!'

'Have to be to put up with a defence like ours. It's as bad as this road – full of holes. Enough to drive anybody round the bend, eh, Nashy?'

'Yeah, and there's loads more bends to go round yet before we get to Three-Quarters-Meet,' came the reply. 'So, c'mon – get cracking, Crackers!'

Another group of cyclists had set out earlier that morning, heading northwards, but with the same destination in mind.

'Phew! Made it at last,' panted Sam, gazing at the ancient packhorse bridge that marked the junction of the Quarter boundaries.

Dan skidded to a halt in the gravel beside him. 'I'm knackered! Those hills seemed to go on for ever.'

Kenny was already waiting for them. 'That's 'cos you're not fit,' he taunted. 'You need to do some more training.'

Dan scowled. 'I train with Wanderers every Thursday.'

'Not to mention all the running off from school you keep doing,' teased Sam.

'Why don't you come and join in at the College again?' Kenny said. 'Then you can play for two wandering teams.'

'Yeah, it's not the same without you around there, kicking people up in the air,' said Sam. 'King Kong can't do it all by himself, y'know.'

'And here he comes at last!' Kenny whooped as Richard Congdon laboured towards them up the final slope. 'Sorry, King Kong, you're out of the medals. Only the wooden spoon left for you.'

'Shut yer face!' snarled King Kong. 'We're not all super-fit like you.'

'I was just pointing that out to Dan,' Kenny laughed, watching the others climb wearily off their bikes. 'Don't think he knows what he's missing, not playing for the College now. Glendale have got a couple of lovely juicy wingers he'd enjoy squelching.'

'Huh! He'd have to catch them first. They're quick.'

'Wouldn't be so quick after I'd had a go at them,' Dan grinned. 'D'yer reckon old Griff would have me back in the squad?'

'Like a shot,' Sam assured him. 'He wants to win the Cup as much as we do now we've got so close – and he knows you'd strengthen the side, despite all the grief you cause him.'

Dan nodded his head slowly, thinking it over. 'OK, I'll give it another go after half-term,' he agreed. 'But if Griff subs me once more, that's it – finished for good.'

The boys went to sit beside the little brook that rippled beneath the humpbacked bridge on its meandering course downhill towards the lake. The area was a popular picnic site in the summer, but in the middle of February, they had it to themselves – although not for long.

'Did you know that people used to play football here?' said King Kong.

'Not very flat,' remarked Sam.

'Didn't need to be, not for the sort of football

in them days. Didn't have any rules or nothing.'

Dan's eyes lit up. 'No refs neither?'

'Course not. Must've been great, eh? You could do as much kicking and thumping and gouging as you liked.'

'Sounds like my kind of game,' Dan laughed. 'Tell us more.'

'Well, if you'd been to more history lessons, you'd know about it already,' King Kong replied. 'It's how football started, yonks ago.'

'*Yonks ago?* Is that a technical term you historians use?'

King Kong ignored the sarcasm. 'Whole villages took part in a game, with the goals often miles apart.'

He was interrupted again, this time by Kenny. 'You'd have to be fit to play on a pitch that size.'

'Dad told me that this packhorse bridge was one of the goals. They had to get the ball through its arch to score.'

'Let's have a game now,' Kenny suggested. 'I've got a ball in my bag.'

'What, a real football?'

'No, just a small one, but it'll do for a bit of a kickabout.'

'Need a rest first,' said Dan, stretching out on the grassy bank. 'All this history's doing my head in.'

'And a drink,' added Sam. 'Who wants some Coke?'

Ten minutes later, suitably refreshed, they spotted some other bikers approaching the bridge, following the ancient packhorse trail from the north.

'Well, well, would you believe it?' chuckled King Kong. 'Looks like the opposition have just turned up, guys!'

FREE-FOR-ALL

. . . stand by for a game with no holds barred, but keep your distance – this could get very rough . . .

'Goal!' shrieked Nashy after hurling the ball under the single arch of the bridge. 'Unstoppable.'

'Huh! Only 'cos there was no goalie there to stop it,' snorted Sam. 'Anyway, we're still winning three–two.'

'Rubbish! That last one of yours didn't count. Went over the bar.'

'What bar? It went in between the trees, so it's a goal.'

'It was way too high. Look how low your arch is.'

'Yeah, but it's wider than your trees.'

It wasn't the first argument in the game, and it wouldn't be the last, but it was all part of the fun. Once the Glendale lads had recovered from the shock of meeting the College players – and from their trek – they had been just as keen to continue the Cup rivalry by accepting the challenge of a match.

'This could be the unofficial second leg,' laughed Chris Kemp.

'I was suspended for the first,' Carl boasted.

'I couldn't even be bothered to play in it,' Dan sneered. 'Knew you lot weren't worth getting out of bed for.'

'Is that so? Well, I hope you make the effort next week – 'cos I'll be there waiting for you.'

Dan wasn't one to be intimidated. 'Might do,' he said, affecting a yawn. 'Have to see how I feel when I wake up.'

Crackers butted in. 'Right, well I can see you two are going to be great pals, so let's get started, shall we? What are the rules?'

'There aren't any,' Dan stated flatly, still staring at Carl. 'Anything goes. This is gonna be football, old-style. You tell 'em, King Kong.'

So King Kong told them. 'Only thing is,' he finished, 'it'll have to be an ordinary ball. We haven't got the kind they used to play with.'

'And what was that?' asked Nashy.

'One made of pigs' bladders.'

They were all quite relieved about that.

The all-action, energy-burning contest took the rampaging participants in and out of the three Quarters, up and down the grassy, muddy slopes either side of the brook and even into the

brook itself in pursuit of the ball. They were soon past caring about their wet jeans and soggy trainers. Reaching the ball first became the main priority. They either kicked the ball in the general direction of the opposing goal or picked it up and ran with it before throwing it for a teammate to catch. Anybody too slow to release the ball was jumped on, manhandled and robbed.

The score was about five-all when Carl and Dan brought proceedings to a premature halt. They had been niggling away at one another all game, barging, tripping and swearing, but now they clashed head-on in midstream. Neither would let go of the ball until Carl tugged Dan off balance and then thumped him in the stomach, but Dan held on to Carl's jumper and pulled him down into the water too.

It took all the other players to separate the thrashing pair and haul them apart to a safe distance. Everyone was soaked and breathing heavily, while the two adversaries continued to swap insults and threats.

'End of game, I reckon,' said King Kong. 'Time to go home and get cleaned up.'

'Are you two gonna shake hands or what?' asked Sam.

'You've got to be joking,' snapped Dan. 'With that hooligan?'

'I'll *do* you next week, kid,' warned Carl. 'That's if you dare turn up.'

'Oh, I'll be there now, don't worry – whether I'm playing or not. Wouldn't miss it for the world.'

'Just stick to the soccer next time you meet, OK?' urged Kenny.

'This ain't settled yet,' Carl muttered.

'Dead right, there,' retorted Dan, turning away towards the bikes. 'But it will be next week, one way or another.'

'So will the Cup-tie,' murmured Nashy.

'Uugh!' Kempy exclaimed in disgust as he examined the state of his clothes. 'Mum'll kill me when she sees what a mess I'm in.'

One by one, the players collected their bikes and began to set off in opposite directions. It was a long, wet, uncomfortable ride home for everybody.

. . . bet they're all going to find themselves in hot water when they get home – and probably not just in the bath . . .

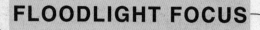

FLOODLIGHT FOCUS

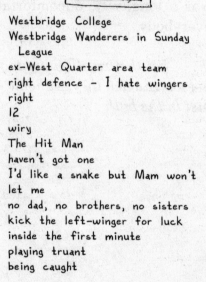

. . . on **Dan Cross**

school	Westbridge College
other teams	Westbridge Wanderers in Sunday League
	ex-West Quarter area team
position	right defence - I hate wingers
best foot forward	right
age	12
build	wiry
nickname	The Hit Man
ambition	haven't got one
pets	I'd like a snake but Mam won't let me
family	no dad, no brothers, no sisters
superstitions	kick the left-winger for luck inside the first minute
hobbies	playing truant
so embarrassing!	being caught

favourites

school subject	you've got to be joking
football team	Wanderers
book	only read comics
TV programme	late night horror films
music	hate music
food	fish and chips
drink	anything fizzy
word/saying	hate/you've got to be joking

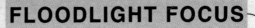

FLOODLIGHT FOCUS

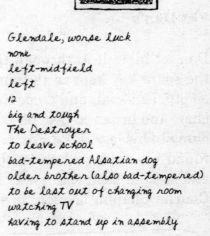

. . . on **Carl Simpson**

school	Glendale, worse luck
other teams	none
position	left-midfield
best foot forward	left
age	12
build	big and tough
nickname	The Destroyer
ambition	to leave school
pets	bad-tempered Alsatian dog
family	older brother (also bad-tempered)
superstitions	to be last out of changing room
hobbies	watching TV
so embarrassing!	having to stand up in assembly

favourites

school subject	none
football team	Liverpool
book	don't like reading
TV programme	The Simpsons!
music	loud
food	sausages
drink	Coke
word/saying	I'll do you!

BEHIND CLOSED DOORS

. . . take a look at the contrasting homecomings that await Dan and Carl . . .

– at Dan's

Dan let himself in through the back door with the spare key kept in the shed. The house was empty, as usual, and cold. He sat on a kitchen chair and began to peel off the filthy jeans that clung to his legs. He'd just managed to get them round his ankles when he spotted a few coins and a note near the sink. He waddled over, Charlie Chaplin fashion, to see what it said.

Gone to work. Don't stay up too late watching the telly. Here's some money to go & get some fish & chips for tea. Hope you had a nice day out. See you in the morning.

Luv Mam

'Huh! *Hopes I had a nice day out*,' he repeated aloud. 'Yeah, just met some maniac who dunked me in the brook and nearly broke my arm. Very nice!'

Hopping about on one leg, he pulled off his jeans and tossed them over towards the washing-machine, adding his torn shirt and smelly socks to the pile of dirty washing on the floor.

'Might as well go and have a bath,' he muttered.

Dan padded upstairs to the bathroom and turned on the taps while he went to the toilet. He soon realized that something was wrong. He put his hand under the gushing taps and quickly withdrew it, swearing.

'Typical!' he fumed. 'No flamin' hot water.'

– at the Simpsons'

'You're late! Where've you been?' demanded Carl's father.

'Just out on my bike with a few mates.'

Only Carl's head had appeared round the door of the lounge. He'd hoped to sneak back in the house and up to his bedroom where he could change his clothes, but the dog's barking betrayed him.

'Mates!' scoffed Jake, Carl's older brother, from the sofa. 'You ain't got no mates.'

'Hope you ain't scratched that bike,' his father said gruffly. 'Cost a fortune, that did.'

'Would've done if you'd paid for it, Pa!' cackled Jake.

'Shut yer big mouth, you. Boy knows nothing.'

Jake took a slurp from his can of lager. 'Why yer hidin' from us? Come in here so we can see yer.'

Carl shuffled into the room, bracing himself for whatever abuse was about to come his way. Their Alsatian dog got up on its arthritic legs and staggered over to sniff at his stained clothes.

'Good grief! Just look at that, Pa!' Jake guffawed. 'Looks like somethin' Fang's brought in from the rubbish heap.'

Their dad dragged his eyes away from the TV screen. 'Come 'ere, you,' he ordered, pointing a finger first at Carl and then to the side of his armchair. 'What yer been up to?'

'Nothing, Pa, honest.'

'Liar!' The accusation was swiftly followed by

a fierce jab into Carl's stomach. 'Now tell me the truth.'

'I ain't been doing nothing, Pa,' Carl gasped, still winded. 'Just playing football and I slipped and fell in the brook, that's all.'

'You're a mess. What are yer?'

'A mess, Pa.' Carl hung his head, not knowing when or where the next blow was going to come. His dad was even more devious than his brother. Jake was more likely to give him a black eye or a cut lip. Pa usually struck him where it didn't show.

When nothing happened, Carl made the mistake of relaxing his stomach muscles and that's when Pa hit him again, this time with a closed fist which doubled him up in pain.

'Stand up, boy, and stop yer whimperin'. Now go and fetch that bike in here. If there's one mark on it, you'll get more o' the same, I promise yer.'

Carl backed away towards the door. 'Where's Ma?' he asked, hoping she might be able to intervene. It was a forlorn hope. She hardly dared to stand up for herself.

'Out workin', where d'yer think?' sniggered Jake. 'Somebody's got to earn some dosh in this place.'

Pa gave him a dirty look. Jake was too big and strong now for anything more. He took his frustration out on Carl instead.

'Yer wantin' to hide behind yer mother as usual. You're a wimp, boy. What are yer?'

Carl groaned inwardly and closed his eyes. 'A wimp, Pa,' he replied dutifully, knowing what he'd get if he didn't.

'Dog's had your tea, by the way,' Jake cackled. 'Then he puked it all up and gobbled it down again.'

Carl trailed away. He hated that dog. He hated Jake. And he hated Pa. In fact, just at that moment, Carl hated the whole world and everybody in it – apart from his ma.

'I'll do 'em one day,' he muttered under his breath. 'I'll do the lot of 'em.'

TEAM SELECTION

. . . the possible return of Carl and Dan for the second leg of the Cup semi-final gives their respective teachers plenty of food for thought – and indigestion . . .

– at Westbridge

It came as quite a shock to Mr Griffiths when Dan Cross turned up for the first soccer practice after half-term.

'Hello, stranger,' the teacher greeted him as Dan sauntered into the sports hall. 'Are you sure you've come to the right place?'

Dan at least had the good grace to look a little sheepish. 'I'd like to start playing again,' he said simply, then added, 'that's if you want me . . .'

'I'm always interested in having a look at new talent,' Mr Griffiths replied, trying to curb his sarcasm. 'But it depends if you're going to stay?'

He phrased his last remark as a question and it was clear that he expected an answer – and a truthful one at that.

'Sure. I'd like to help the College win something this season – y'know, the League . . . or the Cup.'

Mr Griffiths smiled. 'Well, if you work hard, Dan, and show the right attitude, then fine – but you can't expect to be welcomed back like a prodigal son and just walk straight into the team. You appreciate that, I trust?'

Dan nodded. 'Um . . .' he faltered, 'but it's the Cup this Saturday . . .'

'Bit early, don't you think?' said Mr Griffiths and then saw the boy's face crumple. He sighed. 'But we'll have to see. I'm not ruling anybody out at the moment. We've got two practices this week, so impress me and I might just be persuaded to include you among the subs.'

Dan impressed him all right. The sports teacher had never seen Dan play so well, especially out on the pitch on Thursday lunchtime. The defender barely allowed Yagnesh a touch of the ball in an eight-a-side practice match. Their two-goal hero from the first leg was marked out of the game.

'OK, Dan, you've made your point,' Mr Griffiths said to him afterwards. 'It shows what you can do when you really put your mind to it.'

'Are you going to pick me?' Dan asked bluntly.

'As a sub, yes. We've only got a one-goal lead to take up to Glendale, so your defensive skills might well come in handy. As long as you don't get yourself involved in any more stupid bother, you know what I mean?'

Dan couldn't look the picture of innocence if he tried – which he didn't – but at least he managed to give the impression that he intended to be on his best behaviour – which he didn't. He had a private score to settle with Carl.

'Well, we've had our ups and downs this season, Dan, you and I,' said Mr Griffiths, 'but let's try and end it on a high with the County Cup, eh?'

Dan grinned and turned away to head back to the changing room, making sure the teacher couldn't hear him come out with his favourite saying. 'You've got to be joking,' he muttered.

– at Glendale

There was no doubt that, on current form, Carl deserved a place in the starting line-up for the second leg. The only doubt that nagged away in Mr Fisher's mind, however, was whether he could risk having such an unpredictable loose cannon rolling about the deck for the whole game. Carl was liable to go off bang at any time.

In their final practice session, the teacher watched Carl stride forward over the halfway line with the ball, brushing aside a tentative challenge before cutting inside to create space for a shooting chance. Although he was on his weaker right foot, Carl still tried his luck but scooped the ball high and wide. He glared round, daring anyone to laugh at his woeful effort. Nobody did.

'He's done pretty well this term, coming on as sub in recent games,' the teacher mused. 'Looks like he might have to play that role again on Saturday. He won't like it, but that's just too bad.'

He signalled Carl over to him. 'Might have been better to pass there,' he began. 'You had Chris and Nick free on the right.'

Carl shrugged. 'Didn't see them.'

'No, I don't suppose you did, but did you hear them calling?'

He shook his head and scowled. 'They'll have to shout a bit louder in future – like I do.'

'Deaf as well as blind,' the teacher murmured to himself, then said aloud. 'Now, about Saturday . . .'

'I *am* in the team, aren't I?' Carl interrupted then checked himself and attempted to be more respectful. 'I mean, I'm free to play in the Cup now, Mr Fisher.'

'Yes, I know you are, but I don't really want to change the shape of the side from the first leg.'

'But they lost.'

'Yes, I'm well aware of that, too. That's why I want to give them the chance to put things right at home. Having you on the touchline, ready to leap into the fray, might help to inspire the others to raise their game.'

Carl wasn't quite sure how to take that backhanded compliment. It was as if the teacher and the team didn't really want him on the pitch, hoping they could win without him. He felt his hackles rise, but realized there was no sense in annoying the teacher. At least not yet.

'OK,' he sighed. 'But I will come on if we're losing, won't I?'

The teacher nodded. 'I'm sure we shall need you to get stuck in then.'

Carl was determined to get stuck in all right. And he knew exactly who would be his first target as well.

. . . take a look at the starting line-ups that the teachers finally decide upon . . .

WHO'S PLAYING?

These are the teams for the second leg of the County Cup semi-final:

GLENDALE 4–2–4

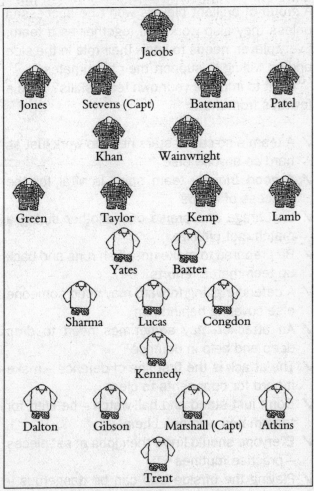

Jacobs

Jones   Stevens (Capt)   Bateman   Patel

Khan   Wainwright

Green   Taylor   Kemp   Lamb

Yates   Baxter

Sharma   Lucas   Congdon

Kennedy

Dalton   Gibson   Marshall (Capt)   Atkins

Trent

WESTBRIDGE 4–1–3–2

Substitutes
Glendale: Nash,   Curtis,   Simpson
Westbridge: Cross,   Small,   Jethwa

TEAMWORK

A group of brilliant players won't be successful unless they also work well together as a team. Every player needs to know their role in the side and be willing to support their teammates.

Want to improve your own team skills? Take a few tips from me.

✓ A team's so-called stars need to work just as hard as anyone else

✓ A good friendly team spirit is vital for the success of a side

✓ Encourage and praise one another during a match, not criticize

✓ Be prepared to make unselfish runs and back up teammates' efforts

✓ A defender going forward may need someone else covering behind him

✓ An attacker may sometimes need to drop deep and help in defence

✓ The attack is the first line of defence – make it hard for opponents to clear

✓ Don't just stand and ball-watch – be alert for teammates who need help

✓ Everyone should know their jobs at set-pieces – practise routines

✓ Playing the offside trap can be dangerous – needs precision timing.

- ✓ Play to teammates' known strengths and skills, hiding any weaknesses
- ✓ Communicate on the pitch – signal and shout advice, using player's name
- ✓ Developing good teamwork needs lots of time and practice in training

WHAT A TEAM!

SEMI-FINAL: SECOND LEG

GLENDALE v WESTBRIDGE

(Westbridge lead 2–1 on aggregate)

Saturday 28 February
k.o. 10.30 a.m.
Referee: Mr S. Murphy

. . . Question: What's brown and sticky and might cause a slip-up? . . .
. . . Answer: Glendale's football pitch after two days of rain . . .

The Glendale footballers were tying up their boots outside the changing room, using the school building as shelter from the rain.

'It's the same bloke who reffed our group game against Foxgrove, look,' said Nick Green, the Glendale right-winger, pointing to the match official.

Leggy grinned. 'Could be a good omen. Let's hope he sees us win again today.'

Chris Kemp glanced round to check where Carl was. 'Yeah, but if we're losing, we can always bring the Destroyer on to *do* them.'

Crackers caught Chris's eye and grinned mischievously. 'When is a destroyer not a destroyer, Kempy, d'yer know?' he asked, setting himself up for a joke at Carl's expense.

'No idea.'

'When it's only a sub!'

Carl stormed towards the goalkeeper. 'Right, I've had enough of your stupid remarks, Crackers. I'm gonna do you for that now.'

The captain stopped him in his tracks. 'No, you're not, Carl,' Paul hissed. 'Save your torpedoes for the enemy.'

'Oh, he's got a few of those saved up, don't worry,' said Crackers. 'If he and that Dan get within range of each other, there's gonna be an almighty explosion – and both of 'em will probably get sunk.'

Paul looked Carl in the eye. 'Just control it today, OK? If you get yourself sent off again, you'll miss the Final this time.'

'Well, if I do,' Carl snarled back, 'I'll make sure I won't be the only one.'

He strode away towards the pitch, pulling the hood of his coat over his head to keep out the rain and hide the stinging tears in his eyes.

For much of the first half, it didn't look as if Glendale were going to require the dubious qualities of the Destroyer. They produced the better football of the two sides, despite playing into the blustery rain, and thoroughly deserved the lead that Giant had given them in the twelfth minute. Robbie Jones, the right-back, overlapped up the wing and whipped across a centre that the number nine met with a full-length, diving header at the near post.

Full-lengths didn't come any fuller at their age. Nobody else had any chance of reaching the ball before Giant. Chris and Leggy helped him to his feet and Chris took the rare opportunity to pat Giant on the head while the scorer was still on his knees.

'Ace!' he cried. 'That's put us level on aggregate. We've got 'em at our mercy now.'

'Another couple of goals like that and it'll be all over,' laughed Leggy.

The Glendale players might all have been guilty of getting too carried away by their success. There *were* two more goals before half-time, as Leggy had hoped, but unfortunately for the home side, they both went to the visitors.

Crackers could be said to be at fault for the equalizer, letting a shot from Oliver Yates slither under his body in the muddy goalmouth. He certainly blamed himself, not the conditions, but not even his worse enemy – Carl, perhaps – could criticize him for conceding the second five minutes later.

The Glendale defence was laid bare by a searing, four-man attack. College switched the ball devastatingly from one side of the pitch to the other and back again before Bax finished off the move with a close-range, powerful volley, hooking his right foot over the top of the ball to keep it down.

At the interval, a shell-shocked Glendale squad were still shaking their heads, wondering what had hit them. They were now 2–1 behind and trailing 4–2 on aggregate. In their present gloomy state of mind, it wasn't easy to see how they could come back from such a deficit.

'You've got to keep on believing you can do it,' said Mr Fisher. 'You've been the better side, but now you have to go and prove that all over again.'

Fifty metres away, the Westbridge party were equally bemused by the scoreline. They could hardly believe it either.

'That was a tremendous second goal, lads, but you're very lucky to be in front,' Mr Griffiths said honestly. 'You were being outplayed for most of that half so don't take this lead for granted. They're a good side and I'm sure they'll bounce back at you.'

'And they've got the wind behind them now,' Emerson pointed out. 'Our job's only half done.'

'Well put, captain. That's why I'm bringing Dan on to stiffen the defence. Let's protect what we've got first and then try to catch them on the break. They're a bit dodgy at the back, as you know.'

Mr Griffiths had given Dan prior notice of his introduction and the substitute was already peeling off his tracksuit. He glanced hopefully towards the Glendale camp and his eyes lit up. Carl was also getting stripped for action. They had deliberately avoided each other so far, standing on opposite touchlines, but their positions on the pitch would put them into direct conflict.

'Just play it cool, man,' Emerson told Dan, knowing about his recent clash with Carl. 'We don't want to end up with ten men here, right?'

Dan scowled. 'Tough. I couldn't give a monkey's. I'm gonna get my retaliation in first before he clobbers me.'

Paul Stevens was having little more effect, trying to get through to Carl. 'Remember what I said before the match,' the captain warned the substitute.

'You keep out of it,' Carl retorted hotly. 'This thing is just between me and him.'

David Nash had also been sent on for the second half in place of Hanif Khan to add his tackling strength to the midfield along with Carl's. That was the area where Mr Fisher believed the game might still be won. With Dipesh Patel giving way to Carl, it meant that Glendale were now reduced to only three main players in defence, but the teacher felt it was a risk worth taking.

'You can't fire the guns if you don't have the ammunition,' he reasoned. 'We need to score some goals.'

★ *Scoreflash: Glendale 1 – 2 Westbridge*

★ *Aggregate score: Glendale 2 – 4 Westbridge*

DOUBLE WHAMMY

*. . . only three minutes into the second half and
Mr Fisher is already regretting his decision . . .*

The Blues were still adjusting to the team
changes when their undermanned
defence was split wide open. Mr Fisher
hardly dared to watch.

Crackers did well to block the first strike
from Oliver with his legs, but he was helpless
to do anything about the rebound. King Kong
had the goal at his mercy. To the horror of the
Westbridge supporters, he slipped in the mud as
he shot and spooned the ball over the crossbar.

The escape served to galvanize the home side. Cheered on by their own fans in the large crowd, Glendale once more took control of the match and peppered Adam Trent's goal with shots and headers. With an equalizer seeming inevitable, despite the keeper's heroics, it came as a terrific shock to everyone when the visitors were gifted a golden opportunity to clinch the tie. They had managed a rare sortie into Glendale territory and Yagnesh lofted the ball high into the penalty area in the vague hope that somebody  might be able to get on the end of it. Somebody did – Carl.

'Penalty!' went up the College chorus.

'Why did you go and handle it?' screamed Crackers in fury. 'There was no-one near you.'

To the goalie's amazement, Carl was actually smirking. 'Just felt like it. Wanted to see how good you were at saving penalties.'

'You did that on purpose,' Paul accused him. 'You're a disgrace!'

Carl sneered at the captain. 'You say that to

98

me again after the match and I'll kick your head in.'

Out of habit, Oliver claimed the ball to take the penalty. He'd already scored three times from the spot this season for his former school. Iain Baxter was having none of that and knocked the ball from his grasp.

'This is my job here, Big Ollie,' he said. 'Just leave it to me. I'll put Glendale out of their misery, you watch.'

Oliver had no choice but to watch. He stood on the edge of the area with the other players, feeling embarrassed.

'Sorry, Big Ollie,' said Yagnesh, 'Bax is a bit touchy about anybody trying to pinch his goals. He always wants to finish up leading scorer.'

Oliver grinned sheepishly. 'Yeah, so do I.'

Bax ran in confidently, knowing that another goal would effectively put the game beyond Glendale's reach. But he failed even to put the ball beyond Crackers' reach. If the kick had gone a little wider of the keeper, his dive would have been in vain, but he was just able to reach the ball and turn it around the post with his outstretched left hand.

'Brilliant, Crackers!' whooped Paul as he led the charge to mob the goalkeeper. 'Absolutely brilliant!'

Bax squatted down on his haunches, head in hands, until someone lifted him up. It was Oliver. 'Forget it, Bax,' he told him. 'No hard feelings, man. Anybody can miss a penalty.'

'Not me,' he replied miserably. 'First one I've ever missed.'

Two minutes later, the penalty drama switched to the other end of the pitch. As Carl surged forward into the area in support of an attack, his legs were swept from beneath him and he crumpled to the ground in a heap.

The referee was intent on watching the play and only saw the defender's lunge out of the  corner of his eye. He was already pointing to the spot as the appeals rang out around the pitch for the second time. Dan was making frantic gestures to indicate that Carl had taken a deliberate dive, but nobody was impressed by his impersonations.

'Why leave it till he was inside the area

before you chopped him down?' King Kong complained.

'He was a bit quicker than I thought,' Dan shrugged in reply, enjoying the sight of Carl in some pain after his heavy fall. 'Still, it was worth it.'

'But it's gonna cost us a goal.'

'Nah, it won't, not the way Adam's playing. He'll save it.'

Adam had to wait. And so did everybody else. There was another one-against-one confrontation to be fought out first.

When Carl clambered to his feet, the red mist had come down over his eyes and the only thing he could see was Dan's grinning face. Dan was caught out again by Carl's speed off the mark and couldn't dodge out of harm's way. Carl ploughed into him like a runaway truck and the two boys were soon brawling in the mud, exchanging blows.

The referee needed the help of nearby spectators to separate the fighters and then stop them from renewing hostilities. 'You're both sent off for violent conduct,' said Mr Murphy. 'You should be ashamed of yourselves.'

They were clearly nothing of the kind. Each was led away by his teacher and as Carl reached the touchline, he yanked off his blue Glendale shirt and threw it down in disgust. 'I never want to wear that thing again,' he cried in a temper.

'Don't worry, you won't,' snapped Mr Fisher and then he stopped at the sight of Carl's stomach. It was a mass of ugly bruises. 'What on earth! How have you got those?'

Carl suddenly realized what he'd done and bent to snatch up his shirt to try and hide the evidence. 'Fighting,' he said quickly. 'They're nothing.'

Before Mr Fisher could ask any more questions, Carl ran off towards the changing rooms and had disappeared by the time the teacher went in search of him. Mr Fisher was torn. As Carl's tutor, he wanted to know more about those bruises. As Glendale's soccer coach, he needed to see the outcome of the penalty kick. The football won.

Chris Kemp was Glendale's usual penalty-taker. He settled the ball on the muddy, white spot and took four measured paces back, where he stood waiting calmly for the whistle and ignoring Adam's attempts to distract him. He knew exactly where he wanted to place the ball, wide to the goalie's left . . .

Peeeepp!

. . . and that's where it went. Adam flung himself the other way but the ball flew past the post – the right side for the keeper, the wrong side for the kicker.

So the score remained just as it had been before the two missed penalties, 2–1 to Westbridge.

Mr Fisher glanced at his watch. 'Only a few minutes left,' he sighed. 'Right, I guess that's it. What an awful day! More nonsense from Carl and now we're out the Cup.'

The teacher decided he'd better go and check on Carl and reluctantly walked away from the pitch back to the school. He had just entered the building when he heard an enormous cheer go up from the playing fields and he rushed outside again.

'What's happened?' he yelled.

'We've scored!' cried Dipesh, jumping about in excitement. 'It's two–all.'

'Who got it?'

'Giant,' grinned the full-back as Mr Fisher panted up to him. 'Leggy plonked the ball smack on his head.'

The teacher consulted his watch again. 'Must be into time the ref's added on for stoppages and that.'

'You mean the fight?'

'Well, that must be worth an extra minute or two on its own,' he admitted before calling out to his players. 'C'mon lads, you're still a goal down on aggregate. Let's have another.'

He never really believed it was possible. That would be too much of a fairy tale to come true. But sometimes, just sometimes, these things do happen in football. Glendale were rampant, drawing a last bucketful of inspiration from a well that seemed to have run dry.

Within ninety seconds, Westbridge suffered a double whammy. Still reeling from the blow of Giant's header, they were stung by a whiplash strike from Chris Kemp. Nashy won the ball on the edge of the area, dispossessing Emerson of all people, and slipped it into the path of the Blues number ten who blasted the ball into the net past Adam from ten metres. The goalie felt like he'd been shot with both barrels.

The College players sank to the ground in stunned disbelief. Two minutes ago, they were coasting into the Cup Final, and now the wheels of their bandwagon had suddenly fallen off. The cup-tie was all square on aggregate.

The referee spared them any further punishment. There was not even enough time to restart the game and his long whistle ended an epic Cup semi-final. The schools would have to do battle all over again in a play-off – but without their chief warriors, Carl Simpson and Dan Cross.

Result: **Glendale 3 v 2 Westbridge**
          h-t: 1 – 2

Teams level on aggregate 4-4

Scorers: **Taylor (2)**   **Yates**
          Kemp   **Baxter**

Man of the Match: **Harry Taylor**

. . . *what an amazing finish! Have you ever known anything like that in your own footballing career so far? . . .*

POSTSCRIPT

. . . scene: Tuesday morning at Glendale School – Giant's 'reward' for his Man of the Match *performance has been to write a report on the game to read out at the Year 7 assembly . . .*

'And then, after Carl and Dan were given their marching orders for that big bust-up, Kempy went and missed the penalty . . .'

Giant paused to let his pal suffer maximum embarrassment. Sniggers broke out around the room and everyone turned to see Chris Kemp go bright red.

'Still, it didn't really matter in the end,' he continued. 'In a weird sort of way, it was thanks to Carl's fighting that we had enough time to score those two late goals to earn a play-off . . .'

Carl wasn't there to hear the rambling account of how he had almost cost Glendale the match with the handball incident and then

107

enabled them to win it. And nor was Mr Fisher. Carl hadn't turned up at school on Monday and when he didn't appear this morning either, his form tutor decided to set the ball rolling and start an investigation into his home background.

During assembly time, Mr Fisher was talking to the headteacher, Mrs Burrows, in the school office. 'I've been concerned for some time about a few marks on Carl's body,' he explained, 'but you should have seen the bruises when he took his shirt off on Saturday . . .'

Mrs Burrows listened with growing alarm. 'I agree with you that something should be done, Brian,' she replied. 'There's a limit to what the school can actually do, but I shall now go and ring the Education Department and also alert Social Services to the situation. Then it will be up to the authorities to make enquiries and see what the Simpsons have to say for themselves . . .'

Giant, meanwhile, was into the last paragraph of his report after describing the crucial goals scored by himself and Kempy. He didn't need to read it out. He looked up from his piece of paper and gave his audience a big grin.

'Totally incredible!' he told them, shaking his

head. 'Remember how Manchester United won the '99 European Champions Cup Final with two goals in the dying seconds? Well, it was just like that!'

. . . So will it be Glendale or Westbridge who qualify for the County Cup Final via the play-off route? Don't miss the exciting climax to the series in **CUP WINNERS** *. . .*

Who else has qualified for the Final? Read about
the other semi-final clash in . . .

COUNTY CUP
Rob Childs

5. CUP GLORY

Semi-Final

South v East

The Quarter Champions of the South and the
East are about to clash in the two-legged semi-
finals of the County Cup – the trophy every
player wants to lift! Who will win through to the
Final?

South Quarter Champions

St Wystans
The Saints hope their new lucky mascot will
help them keep the Cup in the South . . .

East Quarter Champions
A play-off must first decide which of the two
joint Champions will qualify for the Semis.

Medville Comp
Unbeaten and ultra-confident, they've already
dubbed the likely Semi as 'Saints v Sinners' . . .

Lakeview
Determined to knock out their local arch-rivals –
despite the loss of their top striker . . .

Join the Cup trail and enjoy all the drama – on
and off the pitch – in this action-packed series
from Rob Childs, author of the bestselling
Soccer Mad books.

0 440 86387 2

CORGI YEARLING BOOKS

ABOUT THE AUTHOR

Rob Childs was born and grew up in Derby. His childhood ambition was to become an England cricketer or footballer – preferably both! After university, however, he went into teaching and taught in primary and high schools in Leicestershire, where he now lives. Always interested in school sports, he coached school teams and clubs across a range of sports, and ran area representative teams in football, cricket and athletics.

Recognizing a need for sports fiction for young readers, he decided to have a go at writing such stories himself and now has more than fifty books to his name, including the popular *The Big Match* series, published by Young Corgi Books.

Rob has now left teaching in order to be able to write full-time. Married to Joy, also a writer, Rob has a 'lassie' dog called Laddie and is also a keen photographer.